DISCARD

The JOHNSTOWN FLOOD

An Up2U Historical Fiction Adventure

By: John and Lisa Mullarkey
Illustrated by: Dana Martin

magic
wagon

Published by Magic Wagon, a division of the ABDO Group, PO Box 398166, Minneapolis, MN 55439. Copyright © 2014 by Abdo Consulting Group, Inc. International copyrights reserved in all countries. All rights reserved. No part of this book may be reproduced in any form without written permission from the publisher.

Calico Chapter Books™ is a trademark and logo of Magic Wagon.

Printed in the United States of America, North Mankato, Minnesota.
052013
112013
 This book contains at least 10% recycled materials.

Written by John and Lisa Mullarkey
Illustrated by Dana Martin
Edited by Stephanie Hedlund and Rochelle Baltzer
Cover and interior design by Neil Klinepier

Library of Congress Cataloging-in-Publication Data
Mullarkey, John, 1963-
  The Johnstown Flood : an Up2U historical fiction adventure / by John and Lisa Mullarkey ; illustrated by Dana Martin.
     p. cm. -- (Up2U adventures)
  Summary: On May 31, 1889, as the waters rise in Johnstown, Pennsylvania, Sarah Beth, her mother, and Vincent, a boy she likes, struggle to save what they can from the flooding but when the dam collapses the reader is invited to choose between three possible endings for Sarah Beth and her family.
  ISBN 978-1-61641-967-7
1. Plot-your-own stories. 2. Dam failures--Pennsylvania--Johnstown (Cambria County)--History--19th century--Juvenile fiction. 3. Floods--Pennsylvania--Johnstown (Cambria County)--History--19th century--Juvenile fiction. 4. Johnstown (Cambria County, Pa.)--History--19th century--Juvenile fiction. [1. Floods--Pennsylvania--Johnstown (Cambria County)--History--19th century--Fiction. 2. Johnstown (Cambria County, Pa.)--History--19th century--Fiction. 3. Plot-your-own stories.] I. Mullarkey, Lisa. II. Martin, Dana, 1985- ill. III. Title.
  PZ7.M91147Joh 2013
  813.6--dc23
                        2013001729

Table of Contents

May 31, 1889, Johnstown, Pennsylvania

Sarah Beth pressed her face against the window and squinted. "I can't see the barn, Mama."

Mama peered out the pane of glass and shrugged. "It's no use lookin'. The rain's too heavy."

Sarah Beth wiped the glass and tried again. "If only I could run to the barn and gather eggs. I don't mind gettin' wet."

"Heavens no!" said Mama. "It's rainin' so hard now that you'd be soaked through and through. Besides, you can't fool me. You're thinkin' that your baby chicks need savin'."

Sarah Beth remembered the last time the rains had pelted them relentlessly. Her baby chicks had drowned not ten feet inside the barn. Tears gathered in her eyes. Her heart pounded as she remembered finding the chicks lying lifeless in a pool of muddy water.

"If only I'd been brave enough to go into the barn that day, Mama," Sarah Beth said. "I could have saved them."

"Nonsense," said Mama. "We can't be livin' off of *if onlys*. And you didn't cause the rain, did ya?"

Sarah Beth rubbed the glass pane harder. She rubbed it as if she were trying to rub away her heartache.

"If you had gone into that barn," Mama continued, "you would've been floatin' in water." Mama blessed herself with a sign of the cross. "Losin' chicks is one thing. But losin' you?"

Now Mama was wiping her eyes.

"You know whenever we get our spring rains, Stony Creek goes from a gentle stream to a raging river in the blink of an eye." She shuddered. "Thankfully the horses and cows were spared and the chickens and hens were savvy enough to stay put in the hay loft." She lowered her voice. "It was those bold baby chicks that disobeyed their mama and got into trouble."

Sarah Beth felt the weight of Mama's eyes on her.

"Besides," said Mama. "Papa rounded up your chicks into a coop. He carried them up to the loft last night. They're safe."

Sarah Beth couldn't imagine anything safe out in the barn or down in the cellar. Both were filled with a foot of water, and it was still rising.

Sarah Beth closed her eyes and tried wishing away the rain. Just then, Papa opened the parlor doors and stepped inside the kitchen. Mr. Colbertson followed behind him.

Mr. Colbertson and Papa were both switchmen on the Pennsylvania Railroad. Mr. Colbertson had sloshed his way across town and called on the family twenty minutes prior. Papa had taken him into the parlor.

Papa patted Sarah Beth's head. He dropped a licorice whip into her hand. Sarah Beth was sure it had come from the Decoration Day Parade just the day before.

Sarah Beth had loved marching down Main Street behind the brass band. Main Street was decorated with the finest red, white, and blue ribbons that Johnstown had ever seen.

As soon as the last *rap-tap-tap* of the drum rang out, the skies had opened up yet again.

Everyone went scurrying home. It had been raining ever since.

Mr. Colbertson tipped his soggy hat to them and opened the door. "I'll meet you at the depot at one o'clock. Bring your lantern and rain gear. You'll be needin' it alright. Good-bye, ma'am," he said. Then he closed the door and disappeared in the rain.

Mama asked, "Where are you off to?"

"The railroad's sending a work crew up to Buttermilk Pass to try to clean the tracks," Papa replied.

Mama clenched her jaw. "You've been workin' yourself nonstop since the snowfall last month."

Sarah Beth and her friends had enjoyed frolicking in the late snowfall. But, the seventeen inches agitated the crops and caused adults to fall into the foulest of moods.

Papa nodded. "I know. But the tracks are flooded and the telegraph lines and parts of the track got knocked out by mudslides. They need help clearin' them. Trains are backed up well beyond Harrisburg. They're leavin' folks stranded."

Sarah Beth listened with great interest. The depot in Johnstown was a fascinating place to a twelve-year-old. There were all sorts of people coming and going. Freight of all kinds, mostly supplies for the ironworks, was passing through. Sometimes finely dressed men from Pittsburgh would arrive with their aides and secretaries trailing them around town.

Sarah Beth often imagined herself growing up to have her own help that tended to her every need. *I'd have them fetch my chicks,* she thought.

Whenever Papa allowed, she'd ride the lines with him. She'd marvel at how Johnstown was tucked away in a deep, green valley. She'd look at the two rivers connecting downtown at the point where the massive arched bridge was recently built.

The Cambria Ironworks often lit up the night sky and left a smoky red glow in the air. Sarah Beth pretended she was a princess in a magical kingdom when she traveled through the valley at night.

"Can I go with you, Papa?" asked Sarah Beth.

He laughed. "Stay and mind your mama. You don't want to look like a drowned rat out in this storm."

Mama agreed. "After we bring our belongings up from the cellar, I'll be needin' you to go to Hensler's to buy some thread and lace for Mrs. Pritchard's dress."

Hensler's was Hensler's General Store. It was only recently that Mama and Papa allowed Sarah Beth to walk into town unattended. If only they knew the real reason she wanted to go so often. It wasn't because she fancied the penny candies but because she fancied the Henslers' son, Vincent.

Mama held up the dress she'd spent days sewing together. Just the sight of it made Sarah Beth gasp.

"Oh, Mama! That's the finest dress I ever did see," she exclaimed.

Mama pursed her lips. "It should be. The lace cost almost as much as our wagon."

Sarah Beth ran her fingers over the bodice. She beamed with pride at Mama's work. After all, Mama was the best seamstress this side of Cambria County.

"Wait till the rain lets up," said Pa. "We don't want her slinkin' around town like a rain-soaked alley cat."

"Nonsense," Mama said. "A little rain never held me up. It's springtime. This weather's expected just like we expect the chicks to hatch this time of year."

Sarah Beth's stomach turned sour at the mention of the chicks. She said a quick prayer that they'd be safe in the barn. She couldn't bear the thought of finding them floating in a puddle again.

Mama fluffed out the bottom of the dress. "Besides, the summer season starts up at Lake Conemaugh this weekend. There's a social at the clubhouse and all the members will be there. Mr. Frick, Carnegie, and even the Fultons are going. I promised Mrs. Pritchard that she'd have her dress in time," she said.

Mama took a quick peek through the curtains. "It's not raining that hard now. If Sarah Beth sticks to the high ground she'll be fine."

Papa started to protest but Mama added, "I don't get a cent until this dress is picked up. I'd go myself but someone's comin' to fetch the material I picked out for the Pritchard girl. She has to approve the quality."

"Mrs. Pritchard loves everything you make," said Sarah Beth. "Maybe if there are scraps left over, you can make me a dress."

Papa turned his nose up. "You don't need fancy clothes like those Pittsburgh ladies." He tossed Sarah Beth a coin. "But you can buy yourself another licorice whip at the store."

Mama caught the coin in the air. "You must earn that penny, Sarah Beth. You can start by helpin' me get some of our belongings in the cellar out of harm's way."

Of course, the family had no inkling that before the day was over, they'd all be in harm's way.

Fingers Crossed

After Papa set out, Mama and Sarah Beth grabbed lanterns. They trudged down the stairs into the dank cellar.

Swoosh, swoosh.

Mama sloshed her way through the water. She grasped Sarah Beth's hand.

"It's so high, Mama!" said Sarah Beth as she lifted her dress to her waist and tied a knot. "I've never seen the water so high."

"Nonsense," said Mama. "This here water is just like always. It'll be here a week. Two if it gets any higher. We've never had it go past the fifth step."

Slosh, slosh.

"It's already up to the fourth step, Mama. You don't suppose it'll get to the sixth step, do you?" Sarah Beth asked.

Mama put the lantern on the table. She stared at the water lapping the fifth step. "Lord help us! It better not."

Mama made her way to the shelves in the corner. After the wooden crates floated and turned over in the last storm, Papa knew he had to build something off of the ground.

"Help me lift this needlework rug off of the shelf," said Mama. "Be . . ."

"Gentle," said Sarah Beth, finishing her sentence. "It was a gift from Grammy." Her eyes twinkled. Then, they grew as wide as wagon wheels. "Maybe one day you'll give it to me. I'd take good care of it."

Grammy's rug was made by her own hands. She proudly showed it off in her own parlor many years ago. It was green with a gold border and pink flowers. Grammy had stitched a picture of the first schoolhouse in the valley in the center.

When she passed, Mama got the rug. For a while, Mama had moved it up and about all over the house. But she couldn't bear the thought of people walking on it with their dirty boots. So she rolled it up saying, "It's too fine a rug to have people walk on it."

That type of thinking was silly to Sarah Beth. As silly as keeping it rolled up and hidden away. After all, wasn't a rug meant to be walked upon?

Mama smiled. "Grab hold of it, Sarah Beth. Don't you dare let a drop of water touch it. You hear me?"

Sarah Beth used all her might to lift the rug, wrapped in brown paper, off of the shelf. "Can we put it in my room this time?"

"If anything happened to this rug, I'd be heartbroken," Mama said. She glanced at the other shelves. "We shall see. But first, we need to come back and get the rest of these trinkets."

So Mama and Sarah Beth brought the rug up to the parlor and rolled it out. "It's even more beautiful than I remember," Mama sighed.

Sarah Beth nodded. "More beautiful than any rug I've ever seen," she said.

Plop, plop, plop.

Mama wiped her brow. "What in tarnation?" She studied the ceiling.

Plop, plop, plop.

Mama frowned. "A leak! Now where is that leak comin' from?"

Plop, plop, plop.

They raced up the stairs.

Above the parlor was a washroom not much bigger than a closet. "It looks like a leak from the roof above. It's heading straight down to the parlor!"

No sooner had Mama spoken when Sarah Beth shouted, "The rug!" She ran down the stairs and yanked the rug from its spot in the foyer. "I saved the rug from ruins, Mama!"

Mama hugged Sarah Beth. "Well, today is your lucky day! Help me drag it up to your room. It's dry up there, at least for now." She touched Sarah Beth's cheek. "I know it will be loved."

Sarah Beth jumped up and down. "I promise I'll take care of it, Mama. I will, I will, I will!"

Mama knew Sarah Beth would be true to her promise. She secretly had planned to give the rug to her one day. Now was the perfect time. After all, Sarah Beth wasn't a little girl anymore. She now appreciated fine silks, fancy bonnets, and sweet-smelling soaps.

Sarah Beth and Mama made three more trips down to the cellar. They carried up boxes of letters, a stack of Grammy's recipes, a few suitcases, Papa's old fiddle, and a broken clock. By the time they got their belongings out of harm's way, the rain was lapping at the seventh step.

"I'm plum tired from all that up and down," said Mama. She sat down and poured herself and Sarah Beth each a glass of lemonade.

"I wish I could close my eyes instead of having to get out my sewing needles again," Mama said.

Sarah Beth sipped her lemonade. "You should take a rest while I set out for Hensler's. I won't be longer than an hour in this storm."

Mama looked out the window and rubbed her eyes. "It's comin' down harder now. Maybe you should wait. Even the high roads are most likely under water by now."

"But the dress needs to be done," said Sarah Beth. "If I run into trouble, I'll come straight back."

Mama looked worried.

Sarah Beth crossed her heart and kissed her finger. "Promise."

What Mama didn't see was Sarah Beth's other hand hidden behind her back. She had crossed her fingers and made a secret wish that Mama would say yes. For if Mama said no, she knew she'd have to go another day without seeing Vincent.

Hensler's General Store

Sarah Beth slipped on her boots and shawl and draped a kerchief around her head. She opened the kitchen door and jumped into a puddle. She glanced at the barn but headed to Vine Street instead.

The wind had picked up, and it whisked the kerchief off of her head. It made ripples in the huge pools of water that had formed in the street.

Sarah Beth sloshed her way to the corner and turned left. She crossed the street and headed north on Market Street. Hensler's General Store was only three blocks away on Washington Street. It sat across from the train depot.

The pounding rain made it hard to see, but Sarah Beth knew the way well. She stayed close to the picket fences that lined the houses on Market Street.

As she got closer to Washington Street, she couldn't help but notice the absence of train whistles. There were no familiar sounds of the chugging steam locomotives entering and leaving the depot.

Sarah Beth crossed over to Washington Street and was relieved to see that Hensler's was open for business. The lights were welcoming and the door was open almost as if it were beckoning the rain inside. Despite it only being two o'clock in the afternoon, most storefronts were dark. Many shop owners feared the Little Conemaugh Creek overflowing.

Sarah Beth stepped inside Hensler's General Store. She found Mr. and Mrs. Hensler behind the counter.

"Sarah Beth!" said Mrs. Hensler. "What brings you out on such a nasty day?"

Sarah Beth unwrapped her shawl before she answered. The shawl was dripping wet. It was making a puddle on the floor.

Mr. Hensler smiled. "Let me hang that by the fire to dry. Although it don't make much sense since the second you go back out, you'll be soaked through again."

Sarah Beth whispered a polite thank you. Then she spoke more loudly, "I've come for some thread and lace for my Mama." She scanned the treats in the bins. She licked her lips at the sight of Root Beer Barrels, lemon drops, Squirrel Nut Chews, and jars full of licorice whips.

Mrs. Hensler rushed over. "I ordered them all the way from Pittsburgh. Tell me, is she making dresses for those fancy Pittsburgh women?"

Before Sarah Beth answered, Mr. Hensler chimed in. "Those fancy men and women up there at South Fork are going to be the end of us down here in Johnstown. I hear that dam could go at any minute. If it does, it's going to roll right over us."

Sarah Beth paid no attention to Mr. Hensler. Although only twelve years old, she had been hearing about the dam giving out ever since she was knee-high. Adults were always telling unruly children that the dam would burst and swallow them if they didn't behave.

Of course, none of the kids believed it since it was said so often. Even the new pastor at church warned the congregation to repent. If they didn't, he said the dam would overflow and wash them and their sins away.

What most people didn't know was that the dam wasn't really a dam at all. It was actually a pile of boulders, tree trunks, gravel, and a lot of sod, mud, soil, and dirt. Anything that they could dump to build a pile big enough to hold some water back was thrown in.

Old Lake Conemaugh wasn't always the lake it was now. What started off as a swampy reservoir changed when the Pittsburgh millionaires had other ideas for using the land. They bought up the land and plugged up all the spillways and overflow pipes. Then, the water built up and gave them the miles-long and plenty deep lake it was today.

Mr. Hensler grumbled as he filled the grain bins. "It's true. The rich folk built cottages up there that are anything but quaint. Their mansions are arranged in a circle around the lake. I delivered some goods up there last year. I saw boathouses, huge gardens, and a clubhouse the size of a small castle."

Mrs. Hensler nodded. "An engineer came by for materials yesterday. He said they even covered up the screens on top of the dam so the fish wouldn't escape. Fish are all that matter to them. Can you imagine?"

Mr. Hensler winked and handed Sarah Beth a lemon drop. She quickly popped it in her mouth. "Be careful out there. If we get more rain, we really could just float away," he said.

Sarah Beth stashed the thread and lace in her pocket. She knew it was time to face the rains once again. She was only a few feet outside the door when she spied Vincent. He was peeking around the corner.

"What are you doing out on a day like this?" asked Vincent. He was two years older and just the sight of him made her weak in the knees.

"Mama sent me to get sewin' materials. What brings you out here?" she asked.

Vincent stepped forward and wiped a raindrop off of Sarah Beth's nose. "I heard you talking so I slipped out the front door to meet you."

Sarah Beth's cheeks turned crimson.

Vincent took her hand. "I need your help," he said softly.

Sarah Beth's heart raced. She had long hoped Vincent would talk to her. Now, here he was asking for her help and holding her hand!

She thought about Mama waking up and wondering where she was. Sarah Beth's head told her to run home, but her heart told her to stay.

"I need to get in my barn," said Vincent. "But it's flooded inside and my parents locked the door." He wiped rain off his face. "I gotta get inside. It's a matter of life or death."

Sarah Beth felt a pit in her stomach as she remembered her own loss. "You have baby chicks you're worried about?"

"No!" said Vincent. "It's Trinka."

Sarah Beth sucked in her breath.

Vincent knew Sarah Beth loved Trinka. Pa said whenever they passed by Sarah Beth's house, she ran inside and brought out carrots and sugar cubes.

"Pa moved the other animals to higher ground. He was worried that they might get too worked up and choke themselves on their ropes. But Trinka wouldn't budge. He couldn't even untie her," Vincent explained.

He motioned for Sarah Beth to move ahead of him. "Mainly, the horses don't mind the water too much," he continued. "But they've been acting kind of strange today. Papa says animals sense danger coming. Funny, the only danger I can think of is more rain!"

When Sarah Beth moved ahead of him, he said, "He left Trinka kickin' and buckin' and all alone. I'm fearin' somethin' terrible will happen if she stays in there."

Sarah Beth hurried down the path ahead of Vincent and thought of her chicks. "We can't let Trinka drown!" She ran the last 100 feet and climbed on top of an old wagon to get a look inside the window.

"There must be a foot of water in there. It's dangerous," Sarah Beth said.

Vincent grabbed her waist and helped her jump off the wagon. "Are you afraid? You need to be brave, Sarah Beth. We both do."

The warmth of Vincent's hand and the thoughts of her drowned chicks pushed her forward. *I must be brave,* thought Sarah Beth. *I must!*

Sarah Beth's bravery was about to be tested like never before.

Saving Trinka

"What if we can't get her out?" asked Sarah Beth, fearing his answer.

Vincent tied a rope around his waist. "We gotta! All the other animals came out. Even Brass came out without much fussin'."

Vincent climbed onto the wagon and put his knee on the window's ledge. "Trinka will pitch a fit if the water gets too high."

"What are you plannin' to do?" Sarah Beth asked.

Vincent glanced back at the store to make sure no one was watching. "Bring her up to higher ground behind the store. That's where Brass is." He tossed her the end of a long rope. "I'll need help once I get inside. If you feel me tuggin', start pullin'."

Sarah Beth nodded. There was no way she'd stand by and let another animal suffer on account of her being too afraid to help.

And within seconds, Vincent had jumped inside the window. Now it was Sarah Beth's turn to scramble back up the wagon and peek inside once again to see what was happening. She heard Trinka grunting but it was too dark to see anything.

"Vincent!" called Sarah Beth. "Where are you?"

When a reply didn't come, she tugged on the rope. She hoped it would make him call out. When she got no answer, she didn't hesitate to go through the window herself. She landed in a mixture of hay, mud, and manure. *Mama's gonna throw a fit!*

She followed the sound of Trinka's grunts. Soon she found both Trinka and Vincent in a stall by the far end of the barn. Trinka swished

use soiled thread or lace. Mrs. Pritchard wouldn't have it. That would be the end of Mama's dressmaking days."

Vincent continued to stroke Trinka. "We'll get you more as soon as we get Trinka free."

"Your Ma said she ordered it special for my Mama. And I can't let your Ma know I ruined them. She might pitch a fit, too." She wiped her tears. "You think Mueller's got lace and thread?"

Mueller's General Store was over the canal near the ironworks.

"Maybe," said Vincent. "But they could've closed their doors 'cause of the rain."

Sarah Beth picked some hay out of her hair. "We gotta try, Vincent. I have some coins in my money jar. If Hensler's stayed open for business, maybe Mueller's did the same." She turned to Trinka. "You gotta help us now, Trinka. Do you hear me?"

Trinka's tail swished back and forth. She nudged her head between Vincent's and Sarah Beth's.

As they led Trinka out of the barn, Vincent knew he'd do anything to help Sarah Beth. Not because she had helped save Trinka's life. But because his own life was happier whenever Sarah Beth was around.

The Money Jar

Slowly Vincent and Sarah Beth made their way back to Sarah Beth's home. They saw neighbors moving their valuables to higher places in their homes, barns, and sheds.

Vincent started to laugh.

"Whatcha laughin' at?" asked Sarah Beth. She looked around the streets. "I don't see anything amusing."

"We must look like a fine mess and smell even worse!" said Vincent. "Your mama ain't gonna be happy when she sees you like that, Sarah Beth."

Sarah Beth hadn't given much thought to her soiled clothes. She was too worried about the ruined lace and spool of thread to think about anything else.

"Maybe she won't have to see me," said Sarah Beth.

Vincent looked confused.

"We didn't see your ma and pa when we left your barn. Maybe we can avoid seein' mine. My papa is at the depot and my mama is closin' her eyes."

Vincent shielded his eyes as the rain pelted down on his face. "But you got to get your money. How you gonna do that without your mama knowin'?"

Sarah Beth stiffened but didn't say a word.

As they continued walking, Vincent couldn't tell if Sarah Beth was crying again or if the rain made it just seem that way.

As they turned onto Vine Street, Sarah Beth shared her plan.

"I'm gonna go inside and get my money jar. There's not much inside, but maybe it's enough.

If Mama's sleepin', she'll never know."

"What if she's awake?" asked Vincent. "What'll you do then?"

Sarah Beth ran her fingers through her tangled hair. "I suppose she'll know as soon as she sees me. Papa said I'd look like a drowned alley cat if I went out and I'm sure I do. She won't dare let me go back out in this rain. I'd have to fess up. Nothin' else I can do."

Vincent's eyes brightened. "I could go to Mueller's for you if your ma's awake. Just get the jar for me and I'll try. I'd do anything to help you."

Sarah Beth smiled. "But she'll ask to see the thread and lace. It's no use."

"Tell her Hensler's was closed. Then I'll ride Trinka to Mueller's to see if it's open. If so, I'll get them. Then I'll pretend to drop by and give your mama her order from Hensler's. She won't be any the wiser."

Sarah Beth clapped her hands. "That just might work!" She pointed to her barn. "Bring Trinka down there behind the barn. Stay behind it so Mama don't notice. I'll sneak inside and get my money jar."

As Sarah Beth broke off to the right, Vincent went left down the path to the barn.

When Sarah Beth left them, Trinka was back to her fussing.

"Trinka! Calm down, girl!" shouted Vincent through the raindrops. "You've never let rain bother you before. What's got you so worked up now?" He pulled her toward the barn. "It's Sarah Beth's barn. No need worryin'."

But Trinka started to buck once again. "Are you sensin' danger? Are you 'fraid of all this rain?"

Vincent looked up in the sky. "I'm startin' to feel a bit nervous myself. Truth is, I've never seen so much rain before either." He patted Trinka's forehead. "It's just water, Trinka. It can't harm you much now, can it?"

As Vincent struggled to keep Trinka calm, Sarah Beth unlatched the back door. She found herself in her warm, cozy kitchen. Within seconds, a puddle of water formed under her boots. She pulled off her boots and slipped quietly up the stairs. Mama's room was at the top. She peeked inside and saw Mama sleeping peacefully with a blanket tucked under her chin.

She tiptoed past the door and stepped inside hers. When she opened her closet door, a loud squeak filled the air. She held her breath and listened for any sign that it had woken Mama.

Convinced it hadn't, Sarah Beth reached behind an old dress and pulled out her money jar. Three pennies lay on the bottom. *This won't be enough.*

Sarah Beth paced around her room. As she tried to think of a foolproof plan, she looked out her window and saw Vincent struggling with Trinka once again. The old mare looked angrier than ever. What if her chicks were just as scared? Just the thought made her want to cry all over again. After staring at her lonely coins and thinking a minute, Sarah Beth had a new plan.

The Ending is UP2U!

If you want Sarah Beth to go outside and check on her chicks, keep reading on page 48.

If you want Sarah Beth to go to the depot and ask Pa for more money, go to page 57.

But if you want Sarah Beth and Vincent to ride Trinka to Mueller's to try to get thread and lace so Mama won't be disappointed, go to page 69.

Ending 1: Save the Chicks

By the time Sarah Beth went back outside, Trinka was making even more of a racket.

"I'm tellin' Mama the truth," said Sarah Beth. "I don't have enough money and I can't be goin' to Mueller's when I have a barn full of animals I'm worryin' about. We saved Trinka. Now I need to save my chicks."

Vincent waded through the water that surrounded the barn. "Ok, Sarah Beth, let's find them." He grabbed her hand and held it as they pushed through the open door.

"I don't see anything down here but water," said Vincent.

Suddenly Sarah Beth stiffened. Above the sound of the rain drumming against the barn roof, she heard the distinctive high-pitched sound of a train whistle.

"Whoever's piloting the engine is leanin' on that whistle," said Vincent.

Sarah Beth scrunched her nose. "Papa says that when a conductor leans on it, it means trouble. Danger's near." She said a prayer asking that Papa was safe.

Then she made her way over to the right side of the barn where the coops were kept. They were empty. Like Mama had said, everything was moved upstairs.

Sarah Beth climbed the ladder to the loft. Vincent followed closely behind.

"My chicks," said Sarah Beth as they chirped and peeped. Despite being wet from the leaky roof, they were safe. She scooped one out of the coop and held its velvety body close to her heart. "Safe and sound. Just like Papa promised."

But Vincent wasn't paying attention. He looked out the window and scratched his head. "The whistle stopped. But do you hear the thunder?" he asked.

Sarah Beth kicked through the hay to make a path to the window. The rain had lessened, making seeing a distance possible.

Sarah Beth pointed to the house next door. "Look at Mr. Demarest running. Are his animals trapped?"

They watched as Mr. Demarest covered his ears with his hands.

Vincent and Sarah Beth had to do the same. "The thunder!" winced Sarah Beth. "I've never heard such a racket."

The roar was deafening and caused the barn to sputter and shake. Vincent was the first to realize that the noise wasn't thunder. But by the time he knew what was causing the ruckus, it was too late.

Across the street, a rolling black cloud rapidly descended over the neighborhood. But it wasn't a cloud at all.

It was a wall of water!

A wave of destruction collected debris of everything in its path. Within seconds, Mr. Demarest's house exploded. It collapsed as the dam pushed through it and swallowed him whole.

As they watched in horror, Sarah Beth's house heaved once. It shuddered for a split second before toppling into the yard.

Trinka never stood a chance.

The wave barreled down upon the barn and took out the base in a flash. Sarah Beth and Vincent had no time to think.

They started running as if in place because the barn tumbled over and fell apart as they ran. They raced up the wall as the muddied water gurgled below them. Both fell backward and landed on the overturned roof of the barn.

It was as if they were in the middle of a tornado. The water twirled and twisted with branches, timber, planks, and railroad ties. Parts of homes and buildings smashed and crashed around them.

A gray, rainy sky appeared above as they rode the wave downstream. It was impossible to tell where they were until they saw a familiar steep hillside to their left. Vincent steadied himself in the beams of the roof. Sarah Beth tried to stand up, but she couldn't get her balance. All they could do was hang on as their "raft" spun out of control over their disintegrating town.

They scanned the crest of the wave. They saw people, some they knew, grasping for larger pieces of debris that swirled past them. Mrs. Langdon, the blacksmith's wife, grappled with a barrel as she tried to climb on top of

it. Suddenly, a piece of a chimney heaved up through the water and knocked Mrs. Langdon off. Sarah Beth watched as her head disappeared forever under the debris-filled water.

Huge leafless trees rolled past the roof raft along with a telegraph pole. The pole speared the rooftop and knocked them both down. It broke the roof apart.

The wave seemed to slow down as the brunt of it crashed up against the hillside. Several people riding on the side of a house floated by them. One of the men noticed that their roof was about to sink. He pointed and yelled to Vincent and Sarah Beth, "Jump!"

As Vincent readied himself, the man extended his hand. "Now!"

Vincent locked eyes with Sarah Beth. "Sarah Beth! Jump!"

Sarah Beth struggled to get a foothold. The water filled with pots and pans and teacups swirled around her. Then Sarah Beth spied something yellow struggling in the water. It was a baby chick!

Sarah Beth tried to grab it. This caused the roof to shift once again. She teetered on the edge of the roof raft. She steadied herself then screamed out, "I've got to save the chick!"

Vincent leaped to the safety of the house. He was pulled aboard by three men. "Sarah!" called Vincent as his voice faded away.

But it was too late.

As Sarah Beth reached for the chick, the rooftop raft overturned and sent her tumbling into the current. She kicked and thrashed about, trying to grab hold of anything she could. Within a minute, she slipped under the muck one last time. Although she battled to come to the surface, she lost her fight.

The dam had won.

Ending 2: Loyal Company Man

Sarah Beth made her way back to the barn without Mama knowing.

"Let's go to the depot and find Papa," she told Vincent. "He always has spare coins with him in case he sees something Mama might fancy. If he's willing to part with them, maybe we'll get that lace and thread after all."

Papa's job was to control the movement of trains along the endless miles of tracks and through busy stations. He was a loyal company man. When the call went out for "any and all able-bodied men," he never hesitated to heed the call. He quickly gathered his tools and trudged out into the driving rain.

Soon, Sarah Beth and Vincent got to the depot. They found Papa talking to Mrs. Fletcher at the counter. He looked worn-out.

"Sarah Beth! What are you doin' here? Is there trouble at home?" Papa demanded.

Sarah Beth told Papa her tale.

Papa rubbed his chin. "Even if I had spare coins, I can't let you go to Mueller's. It's dangerous out there." He stared at Vincent. "You best be goin' home, son. Your pa was lookin' for you. Your ma's worried sick. She thought you floated away."

Vincent turned to Sarah Beth. "When this storm's over, we'll ride Trinka and Brass up to South Fork to see the dam." Vincent squeezed Sarah Beth's hand and hurried off.

Then Papa scolded Sarah Beth. "You can't be out and about doing whatever you please. The weather is as bad as I've seen it."

Papa sipped his coffee. "The heavy rains are causin' problems along the tracks throughout the Allegheny Valley. The trains are stranded due to flooded tracks and a landslide at the East Conemaugh Depot."

He plucked a piece of hay out of her hair. "We just heard that the telegraph lines are knocked out. There's nothing getting through west of South Fork. I'm needed in East Conemaugh. You're gonna have to come with me so I can keep my eye on you."

So, Papa, Mr. Colbertson, Sarah Beth, and two other men hopped aboard a work train heading to East Conemaugh. They made it to just short of the depot. A flagman stopped them, saying it was unsafe to go any farther. They walked into East Conemaugh and saw that three of the four tracks were in use. The one closest to the river was covered by several inches of water.

The trains were moved toward the depot and hillside. But soon those tracks would flood, too. The trains needed to get moving and get out of East Conemaugh before it was too late.

Papa peeked in the depot and saw Mrs. Cobb inside. "You keep Mrs. Cobb company while I get the trains up and runnin'. Maybe she'll tell you about her new calf that was born with just one eye."

Mrs. Cobb looked surprised to see Sarah Beth. "Why are you out on such a day?" she asked.

When Sarah Beth didn't answer, Mrs. Cobb smiled. "Well, I'm glad you are. I can sure use some company." She pointed to a bucket behind her. "As long as you don't mind the leaky roof, we'll be just fine."

Papa kissed Sarah Beth. Then, he and the other men picked up their lanterns and shovels. They made their way around the bend to clear the mudslide. The driving rain and mud along the tracks made the walk longer and harder.

When they reached a curved area of tracks called Buttermilk Pass, they stopped. Ahead of them, three feet of mud and rocks had fallen from the steep side of the hill.

As Papa and the men began shoveling away the rocks, Papa looked around. The slick, rocky embankment was on one side and the swollen Little Conemaugh Creek was on the other. If anything came down the tracks from South Fork, they'd be in trouble.

Meanwhile, nine miles east at the South Fork depot, Mr. J.P. Wilson, the telegraph operator, was desperately typing a message. He hoped it would be read.

DAM IS VERY DANGEROUS AND MAY GO AT ANY TIME

Through the rain and wind, Papa and the men finished clearing the tracks. Papa hoped Mrs. Cobb would have a hot pot of coffee ready for them.

Just as Mrs. Cobb started to tell the story of her one-eyed calf, she read the telegraph. Panic followed.

"Sarah Beth, run down and find your pa and the others. The dam is about to blow. There's no time to waste," Mrs. Cobb commanded.

Sarah Beth didn't have time to think, and certainly not about being brave. She ran out the door and raced east. Her heart pounded with each step. She struggled to find the men working on the tracks.

Shouting didn't do much good because the roar of the rain was louder. Finally, Sarah Beth saw the lanterns shining through the storm.

"Papa! The dam's about to blow!"

The men stood upright trying to figure out what Sarah Beth had said. She pointed her finger up to the valley toward the mountain and the South Fork Dam.

That's when they knew. They heard what sounded like a roar of thunder getting louder. It sounded like a runaway train barreling through the mountains.

Then, in the blink of an eye, the tops of trees shook, buckled, and tumbled. The sound was deafening. Papa and the men froze for a second. They stared at the side of the mountain, falling off and rolling right at them.

Sarah Beth screamed.

The air and ground shook and grinded around them. The men finally threw down their shovels and ran.

The deafening thunder rolling through the valley was not thunder at all. It was the sickening sound of all of Lake Conemaugh let loose. The South Fork Dam had finally given way and everything in its path was blasting down the mountains.

The flood was swiftly mowing down entire forests and hillsides. Trees, boulders, a viaduct, wooden bridges, and barns churned up with millions of gallons of lake water. It was heading straight toward them.

Making it back to East Conemaugh was out of the question. The mountain side of the track was their only hope. The slope along the track was steep and slick. They'd have to find a path to climb to try to get as high up as possible.

After a frantic search of 200 feet, Mr. Colbertson pointed to a slight angled depression in the rocks that led up the slope. The first two men leaped up the path with their arms and legs scrambling like frantic spiders.

Mr. Colbertson pulled Papa along and urged him up the path. Papa then grabbed Sarah Beth by her arms and they scrambled up the path with Mr. Colbertson following right behind. The three of them grasped at rocks, branches, and bushes as they moved up the muddy slope.

Sarah Beth looked back, slipped, and felt herself begin to fall downward. Papa grabbed her by the neck of her dress as he gripped the trunk of a small tree. He hoisted Sarah Beth up to a ledge along a rock face.

The flood roared and crashed several feet below them. They felt the spray of the water as bits of shredded debris slapped their faces.

As the flood exploded through the bend, they saw the train tracks ripped up. The wooden beams were tossed into the air like matchsticks. Green and brown foam shot high into the rain-soaked air as the flood swallowed every tree and boulder. The Little Conemaugh Creek was consumed by the raging flood.

Sarah Beth dug her nails into the cliffside and was too afraid to move or look down. Papa breathed deeply. He shook his head, wondering if the trains stuck at East Conemaugh would be spared.

"If this gets through to Johnstown," said Mr. Colbertson, "there ain't gonna be nothin' left of it!"

That's when Sarah Beth, grateful to have survived, found her voice.

"MAMA!"

Ending 3: Brave Girl

Sarah Beth walked back into the rain with the coins from her money jar. "I don't have enough for the lace and thread, but I gotta try." She stomped her foot in a deep puddle of water. "I can't disappoint Mama."

Sarah Beth and Vincent mounted Trinka, who seemed more agitated than ever. She pulled and bucked and acted as though she wanted to bolt away. But soon they were galloping along the high embankment toward Mueller's.

As Sarah Beth held on to Vincent, she couldn't help but look down. The swift-moving current of the swollen river raged below her. Then she prayed like she had never prayed before.

The Pennsylvania Railroad Bridge loomed ahead of them. A few locals had walked up to where they could catch a glimpse of the rapids.

Trinka stopped and hesitated about fifty yards from the bridge.

"Trinka!" shouted Vincent. "Calm down, girl. We're almost there."

"Maybe the rough water down below is troublin' her," replied Sarah Beth.

They both jumped off of the horse and tried to soothe her. Vincent struggled with Trinka while trying to get a better foothold on the slippery ground. Then, they heard the distinctive high-pitched wail of a steam locomotive off in the valley. The whistle wasn't stopping.

"Oh, no!" said Sarah Beth. "Papa said that if a conductor leans on his whistle, it means there's dreadful trouble."

Vincent eased up on the reins. "Maybe there's a big derailment at Mineral Point or . . ."

But before he finished, Trinka reared. Then the terrified mare made a move to run along the embankment. Her hind legs slipped from under her. She lost her footing in the slimy mud.

In one terrifying moment, Trinka fell back. Her weight made the edge of the embankment give way. She tumbled far down into the river with a powerful splash. In an instant, the horse was swept away in the mighty current.

Sarah Beth screamed as she clung to Vincent. They watched Trinka trying desperately to keep her head above the water.

Vincent was too scared to speak. Instead, he grabbed hold of Sarah Beth's hand and raced toward the bridge. He hoped he could save Trinka.

They got no more than two or three frantic steps. Then, they heard the steady rise and rumble of the loudest thunder they had ever heard. They turned to look at its source—the valley and the gap.

Two men cloaked in mud scrambled up the embankment. They shouted, "RUN!"

Sarah Beth recognized one man as Mr. Martini, the ice seller from Locust Street.

"Young lady!" he cried. "The dam! The South Fork Dam busted! It's coming this way!"

The thunderous sound was deafening. Too terrified to say anything or to move, Sarah Beth and Vincent stood like statues with jaws dropped.

Coming through the gap was a massive, sooty cloud. But it wasn't a cloud at all. Large tree trunks, planks of wood, and parts of the earth were rolling, tumbling, and churning into view. It was like a massive mountain coming alive and raking away everything in its path.

It was a wall of water!

A colossal wall of water was spreading out across the center of the valley. It was descending on Johnstown. Nothing was spared—not houses, animals, boats, or people.

Geysers of brown water shot high into the gray sky as the wave cascaded and smashed through the eastern part of town. The water and debris pulverized everything in its path. Higher buildings shook briefly before collapsing like a house of cards.

One of the towering smoke stacks from the Cambria Ironworks shuddered and toppled over with a loud crash. Some houses tumbled like toy dollhouses and fell apart in the churning water.

"My house! The store!" Vincent screamed

as he put his hands across his mouth. He bolted toward its destructive path instead of away from it.

"Vincent! No!" cried Sarah Beth. "Come back!"

But it was too late. Vincent had run away from her and was sprinting along the embankment in a frenzied panic.

By now, the first of the advancing water was shooting down past where Sarah Beth stood. Huge branches and tree trunks barreled past her and lodged in the arches of the bridge. To Sarah Beth's horror, she saw death all around her. Animals and townspeople all disappeared through the bridge's arches.

Men gathered along the embankment and sprinted toward the bridge with ropes and long branches. They were hoping to pull survivors up from the deluge. Sarah Beth followed them.

Be brave, she thought. *Be brave.*

There were others carrying valuables. Terrified small children were crying for their mas and pas.

Trains, wagons, sheds, steps, and tangled metal were piling up at the bridge. Each hit with explosive crashes and crunches. Entire houses, or parts of houses such as rooftops and porches, came into view. And there were people! People grasping for their lives or huddled on makeshift rafts, bouncing and spinning toward the bridge.

The houses hit the bridge with sickening thuds and crashes. Three men holding on to the eaves of a rooftop tumbled into the mass as the roof they were grasping slid into the pile of debris.

The current began to slow as the main force of the wave lessened. The bridge became a huge dam. The water turned an oily grayish black as it slowed down and deepened. Survivors clung to debris and floated as they spun slowly

downriver. Most looked sick and shocked. Some were injured and others were eager to help.

Many were dead. At the bridge, rescuers began pulling people up from the wreckage.

Sarah Beth raced onto the bridge. *I've got to be brave*, she thought again as the water raged below her.

She walked a few feet and then stopped at the sight of a dress, once beautiful and now soiled, floating eerily toward her. Mrs. Pritchard's dress! And then she saw a far more upsetting sight. Grammy's needlepoint rug!

Mama! Papa! Her house! What had become of them?

She searched the river and saw Mr. Demarest's home, Hensler's General Store, and what she thought was left of Vincent's house crash into the bridge. It only took her a minute before she saw her own home smash into the bridge. She ran toward it.

Chaos loomed around her. People screamed and ran in every direction. Sarah Beth stared into Mama's bedroom window. "Mama! Can you hear me?"

A man brushed her aside. "No one's gonna survive a crash like that."

Sarah Beth screamed louder as fire erupted from her bedroom window. "Mama! Mama!"

But Mama didn't answer. Just as the fire forced her back, that same man yelled, "Look there! There's an arm coming out that window."

Mama's arm! Sarah Beth leaned over the bridge and reached for Mama.

Mama poked her head out through the window. "Get help, Sarah Beth," sobbed Mama. "I don't got much longer!"

The man grabbed hold of Mama's arm and in one swoop, pulled her onto the bridge.

Mama was bruised and battered. She had broken bones and a burned leg, but she had survived.

Once Sarah Beth and some men carried Mama to safety, Sarah Beth leaned over Mama.

"You're going to be fine, Mama. But I've got to leave you now and set out to find Papa. He might need my help," Sarah Beth said.

"Go, Sarah Beth. Find him. Help him. Then come back to me." She grabbed Sarah Beth's cheeks and kissed her. "You're my brave, brave girl."

Sarah Beth stood and looked at all the death and destruction around her. With no landmarks to guide her, she set off to find her Papa. And for the first time in her life, she felt brave.

Write Your Own Ending

There were three endings to choose from in *The Johnstown Flood*. Did you find the ending you wanted from the story? Did you want something different to happen?

Now it is your turn! Write an ending you would like to happen for Sarah Beth, Mama, Papa, Vincent, and Trinka. Be creative!